We're Very Good Friends, My Mother and I

Written and Illustrated

by

P. K. Hallinan

*With special thanks
to Moms everywhere*

IDEALS CHILDREN'S BOOKS

Copyright © 1989 by Patrick K. Hallinan
All rights reserved.
Printed and bound in the United States of America
Published by Ideals Publishing Corporation
Nashville, Tennessee 37210

ISBN 0-8249-8519-2

Story Link® Program

We're very good friends,
my mother and I.

We like to take walks

and watch birds fly by.

And sometimes we'll just laugh
for hours on end,
but that's what you do
when you've got a true friend.

We do lots of great things,
my mother and I.

We shop at the store.

We swim at the shore.

We rest on the couch
after doing our chores.

We even cook dinners
with patience and care,

then sit down and eat
all the treats we've prepared.

And sometimes we'll go
for a walk in the park
and swing on the swings
till the park gets too dark.

Or sometimes we'll go
for a stroll down the lane
and make up new games
with their own special names,

or "Catch As Catch Can!"

or "Run Just for Fun
from the Hundred Ton Man!"

16

But also we're happy
just reading good books,
curled up on a blanket
in our own private nooks.

And, yes, we're content
doing nothing at all.
But that's how it goes
with good friends, you know.

We have wonderful moments,
my mother and I.

Then late in the evening
as the sun's sinking low,
we'll watch the world changing,
rearranging its glow.

And my heart feels so full
that it's bursting inside,
and I start overflowing
with gladness and pride.

My mother is special
in so many ways.

She makes me feel better
on feeling-poor days.

And she eases my hurt
when I've taken a fall.

I know in my heart
she's the best mom of all!

Yes, she's taught me to care
and to never stop giving,

and she's taught me that love
is the purpose for living.

So I guess I could never count
all the reasons why . . .

we're very good friends,
my mother and I!